Grayslake Area Public Library District
Grayslake, Illinois

1. A fine will be charged on each book which is not returned when it is due.

2. All injuries to books beyond reasonable wear and all losses shall be made good to the satisfaction of the Librarian.

3. Each borrower is held responsible for all books drawn on his card and for all fines accruing on the same.

The Lovely Duckling

Written by Penny Dolan

Illustrated by David Boyle

Crabtree Publishing Company

www.crabtreebooks.com

Crabtree Publishing Company
www.crabtreebooks.com
1-800-387-7650

PMB 59051, 350 Fifth Ave.   616 Welland Ave.
59th Floor,   St. Catharines, ON
New York, NY 10118   L2M 5V6

Published by Crabtree Publishing in 2014

Series editor: Melanie Palmer
Editor: Crystal Sikkens
Notes to adults: Reagan Miller
Series advisor: Catherine Glavina
Series designer: Peter Scoulding
Production coordinator and
   Prepress technician: Margaret Amy Salter
Print coordinator: Margaret Amy Salter

Text © Penny Dolan 2013
Illustrations © David Boyle 2013

The rights of Penny Dolan to be
identified as the author and
David Boyle as the illustrator of
this Work have been asserted.

First published in 2013
by Franklin Watts
(A division of Hachette
Children's Books)

Printed in
Canada/022014/MA20131220

Library and Archives Canada
Cataloguing in Publication

CIP available at Library and Archives Canada

Library of Congress
Cataloging-in-Publication Data

CIP available at Library of Congress

This story is based on the traditional fairy tale,
The Ugly Duckling, but with a new twist.
Can you make up your own twist for the story?

Down by the pond sat Mother Duck.
She was very proud of the four
blue eggs in her nest.

Crack! The first egg hatched.
Out of the shell came a large
duckling. His stubby wings had
very dark feathers.

"Oh dear," quacked the other ducks. "He's not very lovely."

Crack! The second duckling
hatched. Her feet were a bit
too big.

"Oh dear," quacked the nosy ducks. "She looks clumsy."

Peck! Peck! The third duckling poked her way out of her shell. "Oh dear," the ducks quacked. "What a big beak."

Now there was only one egg left
in the nest. Nobody said a word.

At long last, the egg hatched.

Out popped a bundle of fluff.

"Now that," sighed the ducks,

"is a perfect duckling."

The fourth duckling had a pretty yellow beak and neat yellow feet. Her feathers were as soft and fluffy as thistledown.

"I will call her Beauty," said
Mother Duck proudly.
All the animals in the farmyard
came to see the lovely duckling.

"Beauty," said Mother Duck, "from now on you must look your best at all times."

She made Beauty sit in the
nest while the others paddled
in the river.

Mother Duck fluffed up Beauty's
feathers six times a day.
Beauty was very proud.

"Look at me! Aren't I the loveliest duckling?" she said. Beauty turned up her beak at the other ducklings.

Soon everyone got bored
with admiring Beauty.
She was left all alone.

19

Meanwhile, the first duckling
spread his wings and tried to fly.

The second duckling paddled her
feet so hard she swam faster than
any of the other ducks.

The third duckling poked her beak down among the cool green weeds and found plenty of food.

Beauty began to feel sorry for hersel
The other ducklings were having so
much fun. She began to cry.

"Come and join us, you silly duck," the other ducklings called. Beauty did not wait to ask Mother Duck.

She darted out of the nest and
into the water.

"Hooray!" quacked the ducklings.

"Hooray!" quacked Beauty.

Beauty wasn't ever the fastest flier or the best swimmer or the deepest diver.

But she learned to have lots of fun
and make friends—and that was
more important to the little duck.

Puzzle 1

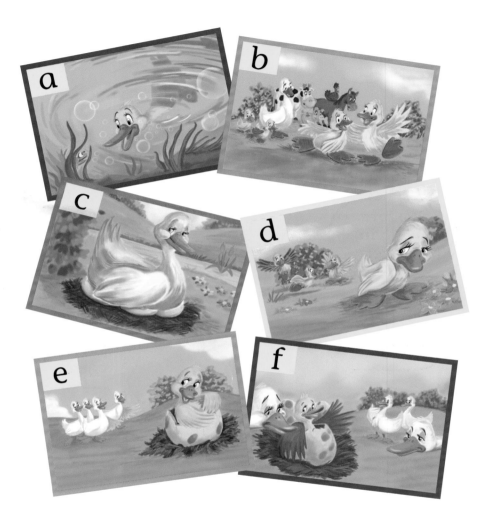

Put these pictures in the correct order. Which event is the most important? Try writing the story in your own words. Use your imagination to put your own "twist" on the story!

Puzzle 2

1. We love playing in the water.

2. You are too pretty to play with anyone.

3. I am very proud.

4. It's fun to do things together.

5. I feel a bit lonely.

6. Everyone should look their best.

Match the speech bubbles to the correct character in the story. Turn the page to check your answers.

Notes for adults

TADPOLES: Fairytale Twists are engaging, imaginative stories designed for early fluent readers. The books may also be used for read-alouds or shared reading with young children.

TADPOLES: Fairytale Twists are humorous stories with a unique twist on traditional fairy tales. Each story can be compared to the original fairy tale, or appreciated on its own. Fairy tales are a key type of literary text found in the Common Core State Standards.

THE FOLLOWING PROMPTS BEFORE, DURING, AND AFTER READING SUPPORT LITERACY SKILL DEVELOPMENT AND CAN ENRICH SHARED READING EXPERIENCES:

1. **Before Reading**: Do a picture walk through the book, previewing the illustrations. Ask the reader to predict what will happen in the story. For example, ask the reader what he or she thinks the twist in the story will be.
2. **During Reading**: Encourage the reader to use context clues and illustrations to determine the meaning of unknown words or phrases.
3. **During Reading**: Have the reader stop midway through the book to revisit his or her predictions. Does the reader wish to change his or her predictions based on what they have read so far?

4. **During and After Reading**: Encourage the reader to make different connections:
   Text-to-Text: How is this story similar to/different from other stories you have read?
   Text-to-World: How are events in this story similar to/different from things that happen in the real world?
   Text-to-Self: Does a character or event in this story remind you of anything in your own life?
5. **After Reading**: Encourage the child to reread the story and to retell it using his or her own words. Invite the child to use the illustrations as a guide.

HERE ARE OTHER TITLES FROM TADPOLES: FAIRYTALE TWISTS FOR YOU TO ENJOY:

Cinderella's Big Foot	978-0-7787-0440-9 RLB	978-0-7787-0448-5 PB
Jack and the Bean Pie	978-0-7787-0441-6 RLB	978-0-7787-0449-2 PB
Little Bad Riding Hood	978-0-7787-0442-3 RLB	978-0-7787-0450-8 PB
Princess Frog	978-0-7787-0443-0 RLB	978-0-7787-0452-2 PB
Sleeping Beauty—100 Years Later	978-0-7787-0444-7 RLB	978-0-7787-0479-9 PB
The Princess and the Frozen Peas	978-0-7787-0446-1 RLB	978-0-7787-0481-2 PB
The Three Little Pigs and the New Neighbor	978-0-7787-0447-8 RLB	978-0-7787-0482-9 PB

VISIT WWW.CRABTREEBOOKS.COM FOR OTHER CRABTREE BOOKS.

Answers
Puzzle 1
The correct order is: 1c, 2f, 3e, 4a, 5d, 6b
Puzzle 2
Beauty: 3, 5
The other ducklings: 1, 4
Mother Duck: 2, 6

GRAYSLAKE AREA PUBLIC LIBRARY
100 Library Lane
Grayslake, IL 60030